P9-CQF-780

SCHOOL

Butterflies
in My Stomach
and Other School Hazards

by Serge Bloch

🌳 STERLING

New York / London

To Samuel and Léon

—S.B.

STERLING and the distinctive Sterling logo are registered trademarks of Sterling Publishing Co., Inc.

Library of Congress Cataloging-in-Publication Data

Bloch, Serge.
  Butterflies in my stomach and other school hazards / by Serge Bloch.
      p. cm.
  Summary: On the first day of school, a student is confused by many of the phrases that are used,
such as when the librarian says not to open a can of worms,
or when the teacher says he expects the class to be busy bees doing their homework.
  ISBN-13: 978-1-4027-4158-6
  [1. Figures of speech—Fiction. 2. First day of school—Fiction. 3. Schools—Fiction. 4. Humorous stories.] I. Title.

PZ7.B61943Ho 2008
[E]--dc22

                        2007043372

2   4   6   8   10   9   7   5   3

Published by Sterling Publishing Co., Inc.
387 Park Avenue South, New York, NY 10016
© 2008 by Serge Bloch
Distributed in Canada by Sterling Publishing
c/o Canadian Manda Group, 165 Dufferin Street
Toronto, Ontario, Canada M6K 3H6
Distributed in the United Kingdom by GMC Distribution Services
Castle Place, 166 High Street, Lewes, East Sussex, England BN7 1XU
Distributed in Australia by Capricorn Link (Australia) Pty. Ltd.
P.O. Box 704, Windsor, NSW 2756, Australia

Printed in China
All rights reserved

The artwork for this book was created using pen and ink drawings with photography.
Designed by Lauren Rille

Sterling ISBN-13: 978-1-4027-4158-6

For information about custom editions, special sales, premium and corporate purchases,
please contact Sterling Special Sales Department at 800-805-5489 or specialsales@sterlingpublishing.com.

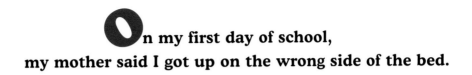

On my first day of school,
my mother said I got up on the wrong side of the bed.

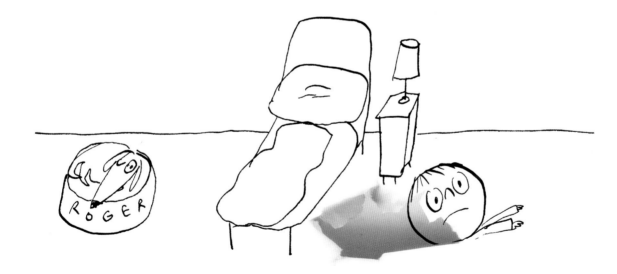

She asked if we needed to have a heart-to-heart talk

so I wouldn't bottle up my feelings.

As I left the house,
Dad told me to put my best foot forward.

On the way to the bus stop, my sister said that on *her* first day of school, she had butterflies in her stomach.

I think I have them, too.

**Then she told me to hurry up
because we'd be in a real pickle if we missed the bus.**

**When I sat down,
the bus driver asked if I was feeling blue,**

or maybe just a little under the weather.

When I got to school, my new teacher said hello, but I didn't answer.
"Has the cat got your tongue?" he asked me.

And then he said he was all ears
whenever I was ready to come out of my shell.

He read us a funny book.
The kid next to me said he was laughing his head off!

Our teacher told him to zip his lip and hold still,

even though he had ants in his pants.

Then the teacher said that if he didn't settle down . . .

. . . he'd have to talk to the principal
because she was the Big Cheese.

In gym class I kept dropping the ball,
and the gym teacher said that
if I ever want to be top banana in sports,
I'll have to really practice.

Soon it was time to eat.
"Why the long face?" the school cook asked.

Then she told me not to worry so much
because we are all in the same boat on the first day of school.

I went out to play, but then a teacher said we had to go back inside because it was about to start raining cats and dogs!

I peeked out the window, hoping to see my dog, Roger. No luck.

During library time, the librarian told us that she loved getting lost in a book, and that we would, too.

"When you read," she said, "the world is your oyster!"

She said we could take some books home, but if we lost them
we'd be up a creek without a paddle.

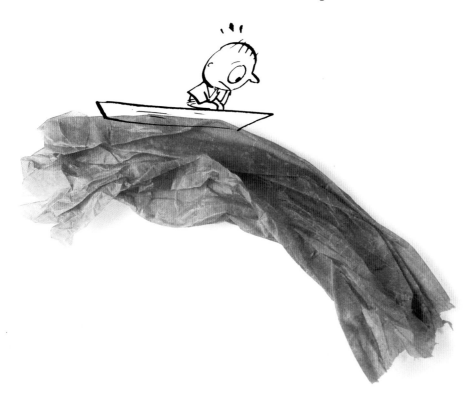

I asked her if she had any stories about a boy who misses his dog.

She told me I was an open book
and that it was fine to wear my heart on my sleeve.

But when I asked her if I could bring Roger to school with me tomorrow,

she told me not to open that can of worms.

I was starting to get a headache,
so the librarian sent me to see the school nurse.
The nurse let me lie down.

She said she could see that school
wasn't really my cup of tea.

I gave her a funny look, and she said,
"It's only your first day . . .

don't throw the baby out with the bathwater."

"But what if Roger forgets all about me while I'm here?" I asked her.
"Let's just cross that bridge when we come to it," she said.

The nurse took me back to my classroom.
"Soldier on," she said. "Tomorrow will be a better day."

"I'll keep an eye out for you!"

Our teacher gave us an assignment to finish for tomorrow.
"I expect you all to be busy bees tonight," he said.

That made me laugh a little.

"Homework is for the birds,"
the kid next to me grumbled.
I grinned at him, and he smiled back.

Before I knew it,
the bell rang and it was time to go home.

The bus driver asked me how my day went.
She said that school was sometimes
a tough nut to crack,

but that every cloud has a silver lining.
I had no idea what she meant by that,

but when the bus pulled up
in front of my house . . .

I was as happy as a puppy with two tails!